Rupert's Tales

The Wheel of the Year

Beltane, Litha, Lammas, and Mabon

Schiffer Publishing Ltd ®

4880 Lower Valley Road Atglen, Pennsylvania 19310

Kyrja

Illustrated by Tonia Bennington Osborn

Author Dedication

To those who seek both questions and answers, allowing the abundance of the universe to guide and embrace them. Brightest of blessings on the path of your own choice.

Illustrator Dedication

To Taylor, my Fairy Princess!

Schiffer Books are available at special discounts for bulk purchases for sales promotions or premiums. Special editions, including personalized covers, corporate imprints, and excerpts can be created in large quantities for special needs. For more information contact the publisher:

Published by Schiffer Publishing Ltd.
4880 Lower Valley Road
Atglen, PA 19310
Phone: (610) 593-1777; Fax: (610) 593-2002
E-mail: Info@schifferbooks.com

For the largest selection of fine reference books on this and related subjects, please visit our web site at www.schifferbooks.com
We are always looking for people to write books on new and related subjects. If you have an idea for a book please contact us at the above address.

This book may be purchased from the publisher.
Include $5.00 for shipping.
Please try your bookstore first.
You may write for a free catalog.

In Europe, Schiffer books are distributed by
Bushwood Books
6 Marksbury Ave.
Kew Gardens
Surrey TW9 4JF England
Phone: 44 (0) 20 8392-8585; Fax: 44 (0) 20 8392-9876
E-mail: info@bushwoodbooks.co.uk
Website: www.bushwoodbooks.co.uk

Contents

Rupert's First Beltane

Rupert the rabbit sat very quiet, very still,
Hiding by a tree on the top of a tall hill.

He'd never been to this unfamiliar place before,
But had heard whispers of its mysterious lore.

On the edge of the forest, was a thick grove of trees,
Elms, oaks, birch, and cypress with their long, knobby knees.

And in the middle of this shady, green place,
Was a meadow, or clearing, a kind of round space.

It was here that he'd heard people would come,
With bells and whistles and sometimes a drum.

Together, they would dance and sing and play,
And then they'd do something they called "pray."

At least that's what he'd heard from many of his friends,
All throughout the brambles and thickets and glens.

None of it made any sense nor seemed very wise,
So he'd made up his mind to go see it with his very own eyes.

He watched, with some amazement, the people gathered there,
Laying logs and fallen branches in a big pile with great care.

But why they would do this was hard to understand,
Why move things about, cluttering up the land?

The people he was watching were young, old and in-between,
With men and women and boys and girls filling up the scene.

Most were wearing pretty clothes of many colors and hues,
There were some with wreaths of flowers laced in their hair, too.

But what were they doing here, he wanted to know,
Why did they come, and when would they go?

Rupert noticed the sun was beginning to go down,
And wondered if he should still stay, nosing around.

The shadows were stretching, keeping him hidden from view.
But he wasn't sure he wanted to know what the people were going to do.

He could see they'd stopped their gathering and piling and running all around,
And now they were all bunched together, standing or sitting down.

He could see one woman talking, like she was telling people what to do,
Pointing to each direction, North, South, East and West, too.

As he wondered if he should move closer to hear what she was saying,
He heard a noise above him, a sudden whoosh, and a branch gently swaying.

He felt a moment of panic, fear telling him he should run.
An owl had come out hunting, with the setting of the sun.

"Don't go any closer, or you'll get a really bad surprise!"
With his heart thumping wildly, he thought this advice was wise.

Rupert trembled and held his breath, trying hard not to be afraid.
The instinct to run was hard to ignore, screaming at him to be obeyed.

"You're safe from me this night, friend rabbit," came a cheerful voice from above.
"I've come to teach a lesson to you, about people and about love."

Then he heard another little shaking of the leaves on the tree limb,
As he watched the owl open her wings to float down to stand beside him.

The owl, herself, was truly lovely to behold,
All decked out in the purest white, with pretty flecks of gold.

But as Rupert watched the last touch of the sun fade away,
It seemed to him the owl's bright feathers turned from white to silver and to gray.

He could feel his heart slow down, no longer afraid it would quit.
And the twitching in his long legs began to relax a little bit.

"Watch now," she said, looking at the people with her big, round eyes.
"From this far away, maybe the fire won't be such a terrible surprise."

"Fire!" thought Rupert, finding his ears suddenly pressed tight against his head.
Those people are bad! Don't they know we'll all end up dead!

"Hush now," said the owl, touching him gently with her smooth, silvery wing.
"This is a time for God and Goddess and all the blessings that They bring."

"If you'll be very quiet and very brave too,"
"You'll have the chance to learn a new thing or maybe even two."

"Many times throughout the year, people gather here."
"Sometimes with quiet thoughts, sometimes with loud cheer."

"To us, their ways and thoughts are really very odd,"
"Especially the way they sometimes think of Goddess and of God."

"For you and I," the owl explained, "there's never any doubt,"
"Whether God and Goddess are inside of us, or how They come about."

"Instincts and the weather, the seasons, moon and sun,"
"These are the guideposts by which all our lives are lived and all things are done."

"But people have a special place in the hearts and plans of the Gods."
"Though it seems they act like carrots, instead of peas, stuffed into long, green pods."

Rupert could feel himself relax, as the owl spun out her tale,
Her eyes now as dark as night against her feathers so soft and pale.

Suddenly, they went from black to gold and her feathers from gray to white,
As the fire the people had made flared up to make the clearing bright.

"Stand fast now, be steady, and try real hard not to flee."
"There are things you can learn if you will hold real still and listen close to me."

"Tonight these people have gathered here to celebrate and feast."
"They worship together, from the greatest among them, to the very least."

"There are many reasons they gather, for blessings, and boons, and sometimes even for bane."
"Tonight they are here, in a circle that's sacred, to celebrate the feast of Beltane."

"Beltane?" Rupert asked. "What is this feast and what does it mean?"
"And why do people come here, to trample the grass that's finally turning so green?"

"Beltane means different things to different people, depending on their ways,"
"Midway between the Spring Equinox and Summer Solstice is when this feast holds sway."

"Some call this time the festival of flowers, fertility, sensuality, or delight."
"The true aim of these people here is honoring Spring at its fullness and its height."

"There was a time when people lived much more like we do now,"
"When it was to the seasons and the weather that they had to learn to bow."

"But times and ways will always change, even for beasts and animals like us."
"And now, with wind and rain, feast and famine, people hardly have to fuss."

"And so it is, that they come here, to embrace Goddess in Her own place,"
"Many hoping to catch a glimpse of God as the Green Man, face-to-face."

"It is here, among the trees and fields, they can feel best the way it use to be,"
"When man and woman worked hand-in-hand with earth, air, fire, and sea."

15

"Here they feel the call of the sun and moon in their blood and in their bones."
"No matter the steel and concrete with which they now build their cities and homes."

"And it is here, with the breath of the Goddess and God touching their faces,"
"That they can feel much more firmly, each of them, their rightful places."

"For as you are aware, my friend," the owl said, giving Rupert a knowing glance,
"Not one of us is here, merely by accident, nor by chance."

"It takes a woman and man to create both girls and boys,"
"With all the troubles that can mean, and also all the joys."

"Beltane is a very special time of year, meant to celebrate passion and love,"
"So that people will remember to take the time to make their lives below as it is above."

"The people you see here, dancing around their May Eve fire,"
"They are celebrating their own, very human and very sacred, desire."

"From shaking hands to caressing a child's sleeping face,"
"Touching each other is a natural thing to do among the human race."

"I think I understand," said Rupert, his long whiskers tickling the white owl's beak.
"Tonight it's comfort, passion, and love the women and men will seek."

"True blessings shared in the union of Goddess and God," his companion agreed.
"Of guilt or remorse or fear, there is truly no need."

"And the children will have their own special games of friendship to play,"
"Knowing it will be their own turn to honor the Goddess and God on some future day."

"Nor is this feast held to honor love only between a woman and a man," the owl explained.
"For love is love, and should be honored, no matter where or how it is found or gained."

Then they were silent, side-by-side, the two new friends,
Watching the people and thinking of beginnings and of ends.

"Maybe the next time people come here, you'll come again, too,"
Rupert suggested, his heart so full, hoping it was true.

But when he turned to look at her, standing in the white owl's place,
Was She who has many names and a man who had green leaves for His face.

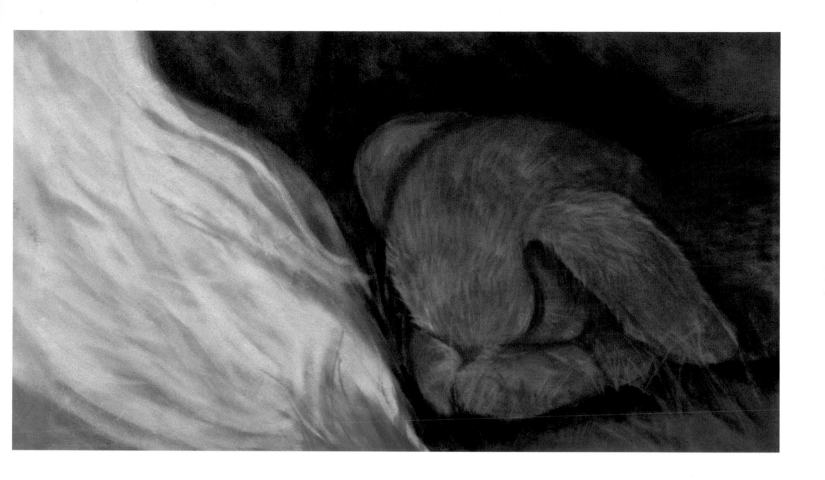

Rupert gasped, then bowed his head, not knowing what to say,
He was stunned to think God and Goddess would visit him this way.

"Thank you for listening," said the Lady with a voice all silvery bells,
"And for keeping this Sabbat with all the people gathered here as well."

"Keep an eye out for our return," the Lord told Rupert with a happy grin,
"For you never know when we'll come to see you once again."

Rupert's Longest Day

Rupert the rabbit twitched his nose, sniffing the air.
He thought that today, he'd better take extra care.

He had watched many people arrive through the day,
And knew enough to stay hidden, out of their way.

The last thing he wanted was for someone to see him,
So he sat quietly watching, beneath a fallen tree limb.

He had seen people in the forest before, a time or two,
So he began to understand why they did the things they do.

Still, they were a mystery, and he wanted to know more,
Why did they come this time? What was in store?

They came here from time to time, to this very place,
This clearing that looked like a round kind of space.

He'd watched and he'd waited, knowing they'd come back,
To fill their hearts with things their cities and houses seemed to lack.

The Lady had once explained, disguised in feathers of white,
How being in the forest helped people's hearts feel more right.

The season of growing tasty things was now in full bloom,
With afternoon clouds often bringing their wet, rainy gloom.

The sun had long been raising his head earlier each day,
And it seemed like there was always lots of time to play.

The weather was turning from warm to hot,
Making him seek out shady places more often than not.

So what was it, he wondered, about this time of year,
That made people leave their homes to gather here?

Suddenly, something sparkled out of the corner of his eye,
Something tiny, with wings that could flutter and fly.

That tiny something swooped, soared, and whirled,
Then stopped itself right in front of him, with a sparkly little twirl.

Rupert squinted both of his big, brown eyes,
Then opened them wide with great surprise.

"You have a lot of questions running around in your mind,"
Said a tiny, little voice that was both friendly and kind.

It was a fairy that hovered there in the space between his eyes.
And he wondered if it was the Lady, in yet another disguise.

One moment, the fairy seemed to be glowing the color green,
Then changed to blue, then yellow, and many other colors in-between.

As he watched the fairy fluttering her tiny, pretty wings,
He thought that maybe she'd been sent to help explain a few things.

"Why yes, my furry friend, that's exactly why I'm here,"
"So listen closely," she giggled, "and lend me your ear."

Rupert grinned and rolled his eyes at the fairy's silly jest,
But paid close attention to the meaning of her request.

"Today is the longest day of the year," she said,
"When the sun takes a very long time to lay down his head."

"It's time," the fairy told him, "for a change of seasons,"
"Though it will be a while before you feel the reasons."

"Time for a change already!" Rupert exclaimed.
He pouted, saying, "If I'm unhappy, I can't be blamed."

"The grass is long and green and sweet,"
"And the clover, right now, is a delicious treat."

"If the season is changing, I'll soon be cold,"
"And the grass will shrivel, tasting dry and old."

Gazing at the people gathered together,
He wondered if it was they who changed the weather.

"Oh Rupert," the fairy sighed, shaking her head.
"Be calm for a moment, there's nothing to dread."

"The seasons may come and go all throughout the year."
"Those people come to celebrate what they hold dear."

It's not their fault one day you'll be cold,"
"Or the fact that the grass will taste musty and old."

"God and Goddess long ago put nature's rules into play."
"So that, in all things, balance would always hold sway."

"There is a time for work and a time for rest,"
"All creatures know this from the East to the West."

"There is a time for growing and a time for dying,"
"Plants and animals do these things without even trying."

"As the season had a beginning, so must it have an end."
"And then, one day, it will come back again."

"But I'll be cold!" Rupert said with a frown,
Picturing freezing snow covering the ground.

The fairy smiled and shrugged her slim shoulders,
"You can't stop the weather from turning colder."

"Nature is nature, it's always been this way,"
"For now, enjoy the sun on the Longest Day."

Rupert sighed, not knowing what to say,
Then asked, "How long will the weather stay this way?"

"Oh, for months and months until Autumn arrives,"
"The sun will still warm all of our lives."

"You mean, the weather will stay hot as the days grow short?"
Rupert couldn't help giving a disbelieving snort.

"Oh yes," the fairy agreed, changing from orange to red.
"Isn't that exactly what I already said?"

"That's the nature of nature, there isn't anything wrong."
"The days will grow shorter and the nights will grow long."

"Slowly, so slowly you won't notice anything at all,"
"Until they both are equal at the equinox in the Fall."

"Well," Rupert said, "that's a long time away,"
"I'll still have lots of time in the sun to play."

The fairy smiled, her pretty face turning daffodil yellow,
"I knew you'd understand, you're a smart little fellow."

"So, those people there, they're happy too?"
"Do you understand, really, what it is they do?"

"Oh yes, my friend, they help in their own way,"
"Giving thanks and praise, they celebrate the day."

"They usher in the new and bid farewell to the old,"
"Even knowing they, like you, will some day soon be cold."

"Without the season's change, nature's balance would be gone,"
"And they, like us, wouldn't last for long."

"To the God and Goddess, their songs are a special treat,"
"And their prayers add energy to make the day complete."

"What role they play, you and I will never know,"
"But without them, the seasons just might cease to flow."

"Oh no!" Rupert cried, a tremble in his voice,
"That would be a terrible, terrible choice!"

The fairy smiled as she raised one thin eyebrow,
"Do you think being cold for a while is so very bad now?"

"No," Rupert smiled. "No, it's really not."
"Besides," he said, "I have months and months to play while it's still hot."

"Then stay if you will, or go play in the sun,"
"It will be a long time before these people are done."

"And while you're giving those long legs a good, healthy run,"
"Make sure you take a moment to honor the sun."

"The moon is the symbol of our Lady—maiden, mother, and crone."
"But remember the sun represents our Lord, who shares Her throne."

"Balance, my friend, remember it well,"
"May the Lord and Lady, in your heart, always dwell."

Rupert Learns about Lammas

Rupert the rabbit, today, felt very bold,
He was sitting near a woman who looked very old.

Never before had he ventured so near,
To those people who often came to celebrate here.

They came here from time to time to this very place,
This clearing that looked like a round kind of space.

He'd learned some things about what they did and why,
From a white owl and a pretty fairy who could fly.

This time, he thought, he'd learn something on his own,
So he'd crept very close, feeling scared down to his bones.

The woman was sitting in the shade of a cypress tree,
With children all around her, as quiet as could be.

Rupert had seen girls and boys just like these before,
They had all been playing and making noise galore.

But here they were, gathered all together, three girls and two boys,
Sitting still, not twitching or twisting or making any noise.

The old woman had a long braid of hair that was gray,
And Rupert was eager to learn what she had to say.

There were many wrinkles around her kind eyes.
He'd heard people call her a crone and say she was wise.

"Lammas is a time for many things," she began,
"You can celebrate however you want, oh yes you can."

"There are those who remember the Sun King named Lugh."
"His power begins to weaken now, just like it's supposed to."

"After the Solstice of Summer has passed us by,"
"His presence and warmth slowly fades from the sky."

"And so some are sad at this time each year,"
"Thinking of the cold to come, some will shed tears."

"There are those, too, who remember days filled with the sun,"
"With laughter and love and long days of fun."

"So, no matter if you cry or laugh, whatever you choose to do,"
"Remember there are many who honor the God named Lugh."

"But what about all the bread?" asked a boy, giving Rupert a start.
"And the corn, and wheat and nuts and the apple tart?"

The children started asking questions left and right,
All their noise making Rupert tremble with fright.

"Hush now, my children. Hush all you girls and you boys,"
"I'll answer your questions when you stop making noise."

Oh, the old woman was wise, it was true,
She knew exactly what to say and what to do.

Rupert was happy she kept the children in-hand,
Because he, too, wanted to understand.

"Remember I told you Lammas is a time for many things?"
"Why, this festival is famous for all the blessings it brings!"

"Yes, the Solstice is behind us, that much is true,"
"You've all had a Summer filled with long days and many things to do."

"And now that Autumn is coming, with its fingers of cold,"
"The days have begun to shorten as the year starts to turn old."

"This is a time of harvest," the old woman continued to explain.
"A time to gather the fruit, the nuts, and all of the grain."

"But what about the corn?" a girl with blue eyes wanted to know.
"My father says it's the most sacred thing we grow."

"All things we plant are sacred," the crone agreed with a nod,.
"So long as we remember to give thanks to the Goddess and God."

"But I'll answer your question, the one you didn't ask,"
"To give thanks for all the things we grow, that is our task."

"Now is the time for harvest, when we reap what we've sown,"
"The time to pick and pluck and dig up all the things we've grown."

"Lammas is the first harvest of three, this festival of grains,"
"Then Mabon, and finally Samhain, as the Wheel of the Year wanes."

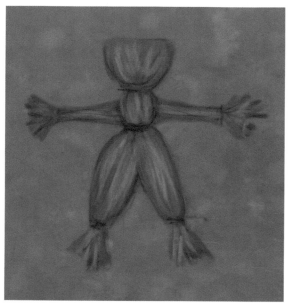

"A time too, my little ones," she said, "to give thanks for all we hold dear,"
"And to remember all the blessings we've had through the year."

"And so we set a special day aside when everyone prays, and sings,"
"To tell the Lord and Lady we remember these wondrous things."

"Together, we bake bread of wheat or corn or rye,"
"We make dolls, build fires, tell stories, and we laugh and we cry."

"So off you go," the woman said, shooing them away,
"Go help each other find special ways to celebrate this day."

Rupert thought the kind old woman just might have it right,
It was good to remember all that was special as the day faded into night.

There would be shorter days and longer nights ahead,
But now was a time of celebration, just like the crone lady said.

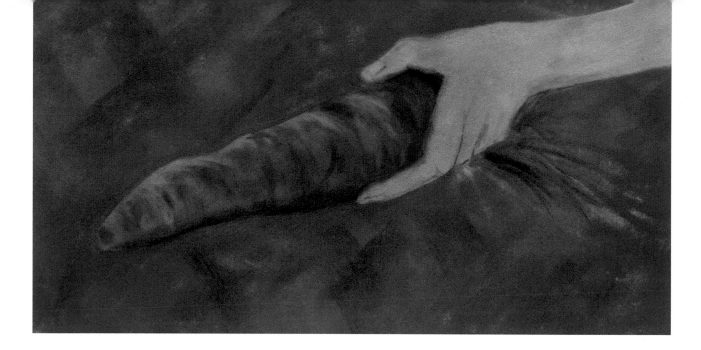

"And you, my little friend," she said, turning to look his way,
"Have you learned what you wanted to, on this very special day?"

Rupert wasn't really surprised when she'd turned her face,
He'd learned the God and Goddess weren't only in one place.

And so he twitched his long brown ears, giving her a little bow,
She smiled, then said, "You'd better hurry along now."

"The grass and clover won't always be this green and sweet,"
Then she surprised him by holding out an unexpected treat.

It was a carrot she held in the palm of her hand.
Probably the biggest one in all of the land!

"May the lessons you learn always serve you well."
Then she was gone, and Rupert heard the twinkling of a silvery bell.

There's magic, he knew, in such thoughtful giving,
And hoped he'd keep learning as long as he was living.

Rupert Misses Mabon

Rupert the rabbit was in a great big hurry,
If he wanted to make it in time, he'd really have to scurry.

So, down the path he ran, through the grass and through the trees,
Stretching out his long legs, running as fast as the breeze.

He knew it was time for the people to come again,
To gather here from all the many places they'd been.

They came to celebrate in a very special place,
In a meadow, or clearing, a kind of round space.

Here, in the forest, out in the open air,
They could dance, drum, and pray without a single care.

Lifting their voices together in song, chant, or praise,
They called on God and Goddess, using the energy they raised.

Rupert looked forward to the times when the people would come,
Especially when they played for hours on their many, lively drums.

As Rupert ran through the woods, he had these things on his mind,
Not paying attention to what was in front of him, or what was behind.

He only knew he had to hurry or he would soon be late,
He'd miss the celebration, and then he'd have a long time to wait.

The people only came to celebrate together on certain special days,
So he hurried even faster, eager to be on his way.

That's when it happened, even though it shouldn't have,
And, if Rupert would have been more careful, it wouldn't have.

Melvin the mouse was in the middle of the path, right in the way,
When Rupert saw him, it was much too late to stop or sway.

And so did Melvin go flying, without even using any wings,
Landing in a patch of yellow daisies, of all things!

Rupert too, had gone flying through the air,
Tumbling and rolling, out of control, and feeling a little scared.

"Are you hurt?" he heard Melvin ask from the bushes on his right,
"You know, you really gave me a terrible fright!"

"I'm sorry, my friend, really I am," Rupert replied, rubbing his head.
"I should have been watching out for what was ahead."

"Why are you in such a hurry?" Melvin asked, coming into view.
He came out from behind the bush, trailing a daisy petal or two.

"Today is a festival for the people who come to visit us here."
"If I don't really hurry, I'll miss the festivities, I fear."

"Ah yes," said Melvin, shaking his head sadly in dismay.
"And just what do you think you're doing, carrying on that way?"

"People are people and not like you and me."
"Any one of them could hurt you, don't you see?"

While Melvin was talking, he started walking around,
Picking up the things he'd dropped scattered on the ground.

Rupert was taken aback by Melvin's strange words,
The thought that any of the people he'd seen would hurt him seemed absurd.

He thought about telling Melvin of the things he'd seen and done,
Of all he'd learned about the seasons, and of the moon and sun.

Of how he'd even met the Lord and the Lady a time or two,
But Rupert wasn't sure Melvin would believe any of it was true.

Besides, he really didn't have any time to waste,
If he was going to watch the people in their circle, he'd have to make haste.

That's when he saw Melvin had a basket he'd never seen before.
In it, Melvin had piled acorns, pine cones, sweet grass, and more.

Rupert couldn't help himself, despite the fact he was running behind,
He had to know what the mouse was doing with goodies of all kinds.

But Melvin squeaked for help, just as Rupert opened his mouth to ask,
Trying to carry an apple, even though he was way too small for the task.

It was a big, red apple, much too large for Melvin to take in stride.
And, oh—it looked like it was delicious and all juicy inside!

"Where are you going with all of that?" Rupert asked his small friend,
Taking the fruit from Melvin carefully by its long stem.

"I thought you were in a hurry," Melvin said, lifting his chin.
"If you won't listen to the whole story, then I'm not even going to begin."

Rupert paused for a moment, because he knew Melvin very well,
This was one of those times his was friend was being stubborn, he could tell.

Sometimes the mouse got bossy and thought himself very wise.
But then again, Rupert knew Melvin had traveled very far and very wide.

The mouse liked to collect stories as he went in search of his treasure,
Gathering food, odds and ends, legends, yarns and tales of every measure.

If he stayed to listen, then he could help Melvin carry his things,
He didn't want to do it, but being careless has a price that it brings.

Rupert sighed to himself, knowing he was already too late,
And he knew his help was something his friend would appreciate.

"I'll be glad to stay to hear all you have to say," Rupert finally said,
Even though he felt sad for not going to the people's celebration instead.

"Good," said Melvin, "because I really do need your help with my basket."
"It's too big for me to carry, but I was a little embarrassed to ask it."

As he picked up an onion, Melvin began, "Today is the Autumn Equinox you see,"
"When the sun and the moon both share the skies equally."

"Oh, I see," Rupert frowned, his voice sounded sad as it seemed to quiver,
Remembering that before long it would be very cold, he even felt himself shiver.

He'd forgotten a fairy had once warned him that the sun would start to fade.
And he'd soon be looking for warm shelter, instead of for cool shade.

Melvin continued to explain, "And so it's time for our second harvest of the season."
"After all, Mabon follows Lammas, so the timing only stands to reason."

"Mabon?" asked Rupert, confused as he'd ever been,
But distracted by the knowledge that the Summer would be coming to an end.

"Well," Melvin smiled, giving a little shrug, "that's the name the people call it by,"
"Those of us who are animals only know this is when the year starts to die."

"The year starts to die?" Rupert asked, feeling alarmed. "But what does that mean?"
Rupert didn't understand yet, how the seasons passed; that much could easily be seen.

"The weather starts to cool and many plants turn to brown from green."
"It's not the beginning of the year or its end, but somewhere in-between."

"People use this day to welcome the beginning of the end of the year,"
"And to praise the Lord and the Lady for all the blessings they hold dear."

"People do these things?" Rupert asked, with a suspicious gleam in his eyes.
"But I thought you said being near people wasn't very wise."

"Oh, you caught me," the mouse said with a sly grin. "It's true,"
"But if you hadn't run into me, I wouldn't have had any help from you."

"You weren't the only one who was late and running behind."
"I should have already had all of this stored, with my shelves neatly lined."

"Instead of taking the day to relax and enjoy all the bounty you see here,"
"I waited too long and ended up getting trampled on from the rear!"

Rupert laughed, along with his small friend,
Still sorry he missed the people's ritual, but glad he was helping in the end.

"But I was telling you a story, and I'm not quite done,"
Melvin told him, picking up acorns and putting them in the basket, one by one.

"As you may have guessed from what you've learned from before,"
"There's more than one way to celebrate—many more."

"Some call this Sabbat, the Weaver's Festival, when they braid bright cords,"
"Casting spells to add strength and unity and setting protective wards."

"And many who grow crops all year long leave a corner of each field,"
"A little bit of each thing grown, a little of what each crop yields."

"People do these things to give thanks for their blessings and food stuffs,"
"Believing God and Goddess will always provide more than enough."

Melvin saw Rupert twitch and understood what he was thinking,
So he gave his long-legged friend a smile while he closed one eye, winking.

"Yes, the end of the year means that it will soon be cold."
"And it's true that the sweet grass will all be withered and old."

"But Rupert," Melvin scolded, "with all we have here, we've got it made!"
The little mouse pointed at the overflowing basket, where his own harvest laid.

"And death, my friend, is truly nothing to fear,"
"Whether it be your own, or the turning of the Wheel of the Year."

"Birth, death, and rebirth are all part of the same mystery of life."
"No matter the weather, from time to time, we all face sadness and strife."

"And that is the message of Mabon, my friend," said Melvin, making a little bow,
"To celebrate what we have, right here, and right now."

"And balance," said Rupert, "it seems to me, is important, is it nc
"Work and play, life and death, night and day, and even cold and he

"Now you've got it," Melvin said with a grin,
"So let's get this all put away so our own celebration can begin!"

So, off they went, the two furry friends,
Not missing Mabon after all, in the end.